DK

DINOSAUR CLUB

The T. rex Attack

Written by Rex Stone

Illustrated by Louise Forshaw

Jamie has just moved to Ammonite Bay, a
stretch of coastline famed for its fossils. Jamie is
a member of the Dinosaur Club—a network of
kids who share dinosaur knowledge, help identify
fossils, post new discoveries, and talk about all
things prehistoric. Jamie carries his tablet
everywhere in case he needs to contact the Club.

Jamie is exploring Ammonite Bay when he
meets Tess, another member of the Dinosaur
Club. Tess takes Jamie to a cave with a strange
tunnel and some dinosaur footprints. When they
walk along the footprints, the two new friends
find themselves back in the time of the dinosaurs!

It's amazing, but dangerous, too—and they'll
definitely need help from the Dinosaur Club…

CONTENTS

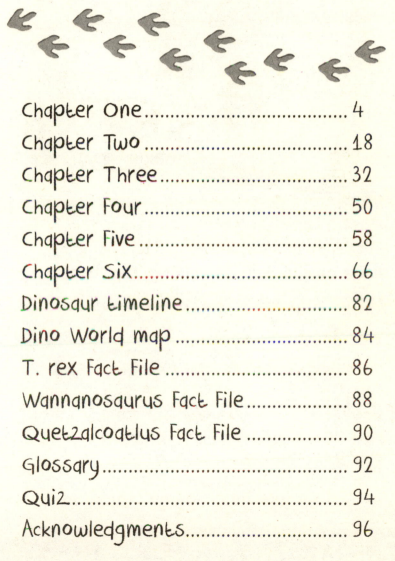

CHAPTER 1

'Ammonite Bay!' Jamie ran to the cliff edge and looked down over the fence. 'Mom says this is the best place in the world to find fossils!'

His granddad's eyes twinkled. 'And the best place for a dinosaur fan like you,' he said. 'Why don't you go and have a look?'

'Dinosaurs, here I come!' Jamie said.

'See you later, Granddad.'

Jamie scrambled down the rocky path from the old lighthouse onto the sand. Farther up the beach were pebbles and rocks, and at the foot of the cliff was sludgy black mud.

That was the place to find fossils.

He scrambled over and the mud stuck to his sneakers. Jamie picked through the rocks. Some of them were crumbly, and he broke them with his fingers to check inside for fossils. Others were too hard to break open.

He spotted a large blue-gray rock with a crack down the middle and dumped his backpack on the mud beside it. He dug out his safety goggles, his rock hammer, and chisel. Then he got to work, angling the chisel into the crack and tapping it with his hammer. He tapped again. He tapped harder.

A stone chip pinged off Jamie's goggles as the rock split cleanly in two.

'Wow!' Jamie said.

Sticking out of one half of the rock was a thin, smooth fossil like the pointed end of a spear. He measured it with the ruler edge of his chisel.

'Wonder what it is?' he murmured. The bay was named after ammonites, so he knew there must be lots of ammonite fossils around—but those were spiral shells.

When he tried to pick the fossil out for a closer look, it was stuck fast in the rock.

The Dinosaur Club will know, Jamie thought. He dug into his backpack and took out his tablet.

The Dinosaur Club was a network of kids around the world who shared their dinosaur knowledge. They helped each other identify fossils, posted new dino discoveries, and talked about anything prehistoric. Jamie never went anywhere without his tablet, just in case he needed to contact the club.

He tapped the dinosaur footprint icon that opened the club's app, then scanned the fossil with the tablet's camera.

'Anyone know what this is?'

The screen pinged with messages as the Dinosaur Club members responded.

'Maybe a kind of claw?' said one.

Beside it was a profile picture of a girl, with her name and location—Lin in Shanghai.

'Could be a tooth,' suggested a boy named Ramesh, who lived in Delhi. 'But I'm not sure...'

Nobody seemed to know. Jamie was about to close the app when another message appeared.

'It's a belemnite. It's a prehistoric sea creature that was a bit like a squid. The fossil is from its tail.'

This message was from a girl with a freckly face named Tess.

'Cool, thanks!' Jamie typed.

As he pressed send, he noticed something—Tess's location was Ammonite Bay!

A thrill of excitement ran through Jamie. He looked around the beach. Was Tess here too? He'd never met anyone from the Dinosaur Club in real life before. But he couldn't see anyone else.

He took out his new T. rex notebook and began to sketch his first discovery.

He added in the squid-like tentacles and big eye that the creature would have had when it was alive.

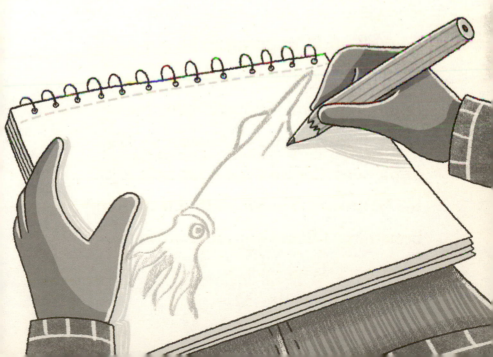

Suddenly, an unfamiliar voice shouted, 'BOO!'

A face popped up from behind the rock. 'Gotcha! You didn't hear me coming, did you?' The girl stood up. She wore a crocodile T-shirt and safari shorts, which were plastered in mud, and she had messy hair and freckles—just like her profile picture... 'You're Tess!' said Jamie.

The girl grinned. 'That's right. I'm Tess Clay,' she said. 'I'm learning to track animals and I'm going to be a wildlife television host one day. You must be Jamie! You're new around here, right?'

'I've just moved to Ammonite Bay,' Jamie said. 'Thanks for your help with the belemnite. I want to find a dinosaur bone next. Dinosaurs are awesome!'

Tess looked at Jamie's notebook and laughed. 'T. rex rules!' She put her binoculars to her eyes. 'Sometimes I pretend I'm tracking dinosaurs…' Her binoculars flashed in the sunshine as she turned them on Jamie.

Tess grinned. 'Hey, do you want to know a secret about Ammonite Bay?'

'You bet!' said Jamie.

'Then follow me. There's no time to lose.' Tess headed off across the beach.

Jamie stuffed his fossil hunting gear into his backpack and ran after his new friend.

'Why are we hurrying?' Jamie asked.

'The path up the cliff gets cut off at high tide,' Tess said. 'So we'll have to get back before then.'

Tess led Jamie onto a narrow path up a cliff and at the highest point on the path, Jamie stopped to look at the view. He could see Granddad talking to some surfers.

'That's my house,' Jamie told Tess, pointing to the tall whitewashed tower at the top of the cliffs on the opposite side of the beach.

Tess looked surprised. 'The lighthouse? That's where Commander Morgan lives. He runs the coast guard.'

'Commander Morgan is my granddad,' Jamie explained. 'My mom moved us down here and she's turning the bottom floor into a dinosaur museum. She's a paleontologist—a dinosaur scientist.'

'Cool!' said Tess. She bent to pick up a piece of driftwood and tapped the stick on the rocky wall behind them. 'We've got to get up there.'

Jamie looked up at the huge pile of boulders. 'I love climbing!'

Together they climbed up the boulders. Once Jamie hauled himself onto the huge stone at the top he asked, 'So, where's the big secret?'

'Right behind you,' Tess told him.

Jamie spun around. Behind the boulder and hidden from the bay was a gaping dark hollow.

'A secret cave!' Jamie gasped.

CHAPTER 2

'It's a smugglers' cave,' Tess told Jamie. 'It hasn't been used for a hundred years.'

Jamie stepped into the dark cave and dug his hand into his backpack, pulling out his flashlight.

'This is where the smugglers stored their stolen treasure,' Tess said. 'You can see the marks from their lamps.'

Jamie flicked on his flashlight and

shined it over the rock walls. He could make out sooty black streaks. Tess took a few more steps into the cave and knocked on the back wall. 'It's a dead end.'

Jamie shined his flashlight over the floor and saw a spider with spindly legs. He followed it in the beam as it skittered into the corner and then disappeared into a hole.

'It can't be a dead end,' Jamie said. 'Look!'

The hole began at the cave floor and went up to the height of his knees. It was wide at the bottom, but very narrow at the top.

'How did I miss that?' Tess said. 'I've been in here lots of times.'

'It's big enough to squeeze through.' Jamie knelt and pushed his backpack through the gap. 'I'm going in.' He wriggled through the gap, shining his flashlight into the darkness.

'Wait for me!' yelled Tess.

It was colder and pitch black inside the second chamber. Jamie shined his flashlight over the walls, ceiling, and floor. There was no sign of any soot from smugglers' lamps.

'We must be the first people to come in here for hundreds of years,' Tess murmured.

'Thousands of years!' said Jamie.

'Millions!' said Tess.

'Hey, what's this?' Jamie's flashlight beam fell on a scoop in the stone next to his feet. He knelt down and traced his finger around the clover-shaped indent. It looked just like the Dinosaur Club icon.

'I think this could be a fossil,' Jamie announced, excitement tingling through him.

Jamie rummaged excitedly in his bag for his tablet. He opened the DinoData section of the Dinosaur Club app. Images of dinosaur footprints glowed in the darkness. 'Yes, it's a fossilized dinosaur footprint!'

'Wow,' Tess said, looking from the screen to the cave floor. 'Those are really rare!'

Jamie saw a second scoop at the edge of the beam of light. 'Look! There's another… and another… Five altogether. They go straight into that wall of rock.'

Jamie could hardly believe it. On his very first day in Ammonite Bay, he had found the fossilized tracks of a dinosaur!

Jamie carefully placed his left foot onto the first print, completely covering it. 'Whoever it belongs to, it's pretty small!' He swung his right foot onto the next print.

Tess was following behind him. 'We're tracking dinosaurs! Left foot. Right foot.'

A crack of light appeared in the cave wall.

'Left foot…' said Jamie. The light brightened as the crack widened. Jamie put his right foot forward to take another step, and he was dazzled by a sudden flash of light. He covered his eyes with his hands. When he put his foot down, the ground felt spongy.

Cautiously, he took his hands away from his eyes.

Jamie wasn't in the small dark chamber anymore. He was in a sunny cave with a wall of stone behind him. The footprints were still there—only they weren't fossils anymore. They were fresh!

He looked back just in time to see Tess appear behind him—right through the wall of stone!

'Where are we?' Tess asked.

'I don't know,' Jamie said, looking around at the strange new place.

Jamie walked out of the cave and the ground squelched beneath his feet. The area was thick with trees and vines, so he couldn't see very far.

'These trees are weird.' Jamie pulled
an apricot-like fruit from a cluster
hanging on a nearby branch. It smelled
horrible. 'Yuck! Dare you to smell it, Tess.'

Tess took a huge sniff. 'It smells like
puke!' she gasped. Then she grinned.
'Dare you to take a bite.'

'No way!' said Jamie, shaking his head.

The ground was slimed with the stinky orange outer pulp of the fruit that had fallen off the tree. Jamie picked up a fan-shaped leaf from the tree. 'You know, I think I've seen this somewhere before.'

He dug out his tablet and typed 'prehistoric leaf' into DinoData. The next moment, pictures of leaves appeared on the screen. Jamie clicked on the one that looked the same as the leaf in his hand.

'Ginkgo: a "living fossil,"' an electronic voice said. *'Rare today, but common in dinosaur times; sometimes known as a stink bomb tree.'*

'No kidding,' said Tess. 'Let's get some fresh air!' She pushed aside a tangle of creepers with her stick. 'What's through here?'

'Wait for me!' Jamie hurriedly sealed a few ginkgo fruits into a plastic bag, stuffed them and his tablet back into his backpack, and then crashed through the undergrowth after Tess.

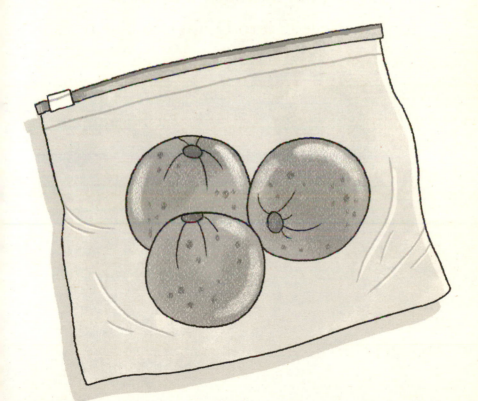

'Careful!' Tess shouted to him from up ahead.

The ground sloped steeply and Jamie tried to slow down, but his sneakers were caked with slippery ginkgo pulp!

'I can't stop!' Jamie yelled as he skidded toward the edge of a cliff.

CHAPTER 3

Tess thrust out the end of her stick. 'Grab this, Jamie!' she shouted.

Jamie threw out his arm and caught hold as one foot went over the edge. He wobbled, and then steadied himself. 'Thanks! That was close!'

Jamie stepped back from the cliff edge and looked at the landscape in front of him. Gray mist hung over a forest of brilliant emerald green. The humid air throbbed with the whirring and buzzing of insects.

'Where is this?' he gasped. Among the trees, Jamie saw a beautiful blue lagoon and beyond that was an expanse of water. 'Is that Ammonite Bay?'

'No way,' said Tess, looking through her binoculars. 'That's an ocean.'

Ark! Ark! Ark!

The sudden noise came out of the sky behind them and Jamie turned to see a scarlet-headed bird the size of a small airplane swooping toward them.

'Watch out!' he yelled to Tess.

They ducked as silver-gray leathery wings swept right over their heads. Tess followed the bird with her binoculars.

'It's flying over the jungle! It's settling on a tree by the lagoon,' she told Jamie. 'Take a look! It's huge!'

She thrust the binoculars at Jamie. Jamie looked toward the lagoon and his jaw dropped open. He couldn't believe his eyes!

'What can you see?' Tess asked.

'I can see,' Jamie spoke carefully, 'two rhinoceroses at the edge of the lagoon, but instead of one big horn, they have three. Which means,' he whispered, 'that they're not rhinos… They're Triceratops!'

'What?' Tess said. 'Let me see!'

Jamie passed back the binoculars.

'You're right,' Tess said. 'And that huge bird is not a bird. It's a pterosaur!'

The two friends looked at each other in amazement.

'DINOSAURS!' they yelled together, punching the air.

'But how…?' Tess stuttered.

'I don't know,' yelled Jamie. 'But we've got to get closer!'

'Over there,' said Tess. 'There's a slope down to the jungle.'

The two of them scrambled and skidded down the hill, and soon, their feet sank into the spongy floor. Great conifers towered above them and huge ferns brushed damply against their legs as they passed. An enormous frill of purple and yellow-spotted fungus caught Jamie's eye. It sprouted from a rotten tree stump.

'This is unreal!' Jamie said. 'I can't wait to tell the rest of the Dinosaur Club.'

But then, on the far side of the fungus, the ferns began to rustle.

Grunk.

'Did you hear that?' Jamie whispered.

'What?' Tess stood still.

The ferns swished. Grunk.

'That!' Jamie hissed. 'There's something there!'

Jamie and Tess ducked down behind the tree stump, and then slowly peeked out from behind the fungus.

The noises were coming from a plump scaly creature with a flat bony head and splotchy green-brown

markings. It was standing on two strong legs, peering hopefully into a tree.

'It's a little dinosaur!' Jamie whispered.

As they watched, the little dinosaur grabbed hold of the conifer with its claws, steadying itself by digging its long, bristly tail into the ground. Then it shook the tree as hard as its short arms would allow it to. The little dinosaur's tail twitched and it grunked softly to itself.

'He's thinking,' Tess murmured.

'He's so cool!' Jamie breathed.

The dinosaur took a few steps back. He lowered his bony head and charged straight at the tree.

Thwack!

The flat top of the
dinosaur's head hit the tree
trunk and the conifer shook.
'He's strong,' said Tess.
'Do you think he's
dangerous?' Jamie asked.

Tess looked at Jamie. 'We should ask the Dinosaur Club. The others aren't going to believe this!' She pulled out her tablet from her bag and snapped a photo of the dinosaur.

'Hi from the Cretaceous period...' Tess typed. 'Anyone know if we're about to be lunch?'

Immediately her tablet buzzed with incoming messages.

'WOW!!!'

'How did you get there?'

'AMAZING!'

'He's a Wannanosaurus,' Lin's message said. 'So cool!!! Don't worry—you're not on the menu. He's a herbivore.'

'Phew,' said Jamie. 'He just eats plants.'

'Scientists don't know what Wannanosaurus used their hard skulls for,' said Paul from France. 'It might have been for fighting.'

The little dinosaur took another run up and rammed the tree again with the top of its head.

'He's trying to pick a fight with
the tree!' Tess laughed.

At the sound of Tess's laughter,
the dinosaur cocked his head to one side.
He turned and blinked at Tess.

'You've hurt his feelings,' Jamie said,
standing up beside Tess.

'Sorry, Wanna,' Tess told the little
dinosaur. *Tell you about everything later,* she
typed to the Dinosaur Club, and put her
tablet back in her bag.

The Wannanosaurus blinked at Tess
and then at Jamie. He took three big
steps away from the tree and shifted his
weight from foot to foot.

'He's revving up,' said Jamie.

'Go, Wanna, go!' they shouted.

The Wannanosaurus put its head down

and hurtled toward the tree.

Thwack!

The tree wobbled.

Plunk!

A single pine cone dropped
to the ground. The dinosaur
stuffed it into his mouth and
looked happily at the two
friends. Then he wagged his tail
and scurried off on his hind legs.

'Let's track him!' said Tess.

'Just a minute...' Jamie carved a 'W'
into the tree stump with his rock hammer.
'So we remember where we met Wanna.'

'Now, which way did he go?' asked Jamie,
as they clambered over the tree.

Tess looked around at the trampled
plants. 'He flattens the ferns as he walks on
them,' Tess said. 'We can follow his trail.'

The little dinosaur's trail led to a small clearing and they found him standing on his hind legs, munching a leaf. He turned toward them and lowered his flat bony head.

'Uh oh,' said Tess. 'He might charge us!'

'It's okay, Wanna. We're not predators.' Jamie put his backpack on the ground and took out his bag of stinky ginkgo fruit. He rolled one toward the Wannanosaurus. The dinosaur sniffed at the fruit.

'He can't possibly want to eat that,' said Tess, holding her nose.

The Wannanosaurus looked down his snout at Tess, then he pinned the fruit between his claws and sunk his teeth into it. He made grunking noises as stinky ginkgo juice dribbled down his chin.

'Yum yum!' Jamie grimaced as the dinosaur slurped up every disgusting drop.

The Wannanosaurus looked at Jamie. Then he looked at Jamie's backpack and wagged his tail.

Suddenly, in mid wag, the little dinosaur froze.

The jungle went still. Even the insects stopped buzzing. The ground trembled beneath their feet.

'Something's coming' whispered Jamie. 'Something big…'

CHAPTER 4

Thump!

The ground shook. The Wannanosaurus
dashed behind the leafy tree.

Thump!

A stronger tremor shook the ground.
The Wannanosaurus peeked out from
behind a branch and bobbed his head
up and down.

In the distance, wood was snapping and cracking. The tremors were getting stronger.

'Whatever it is, it's coming our way,' Jamie said.

'Fast,' added Tess.

They looked at each other.

'We've got to get out of here!' Jamie yelled.

'Which way?'

Suddenly, Jamie's bag was yanked off his back. Jamie spun around and saw the Wannanosaurus charging into the jungle, clutching it in his mouth.

'Wanna!' Jamie sprinted after him, with Tess close behind.

The little dinosaur skidded to a halt by
a shallow stream. He turned and looked
Jamie in the eyes. Then he jerked his head
toward the stream and plunged in.

The ground shook again.

'Wanna's leading us to safety!' Jamie
shouted, jumping into the stream after him.

'Smart!' Tess panted. 'The water will
mask our scent.'

Wanna led them up the stream
to where it trickled through a
jumble of huge rounded rocks.
He glanced back and leaped out
of the water.

Jamie and Tess followed, stumbling
and splashing. They scrambled onto the
rocks and stood, dripping.

'Where'd he go?' Jamie said.

RAAAR!

Something crashed through the trees behind them. Jamie whirled around and lost his footing on the wet stone.

He grabbed onto Tess's stick to steady himself, but this time the stick came away and fell into the water as they both toppled and slid down between two rocks. Jamie landed with a thud and found himself staring into a reptilian face.

Grunk!

Wanna greeted Jamie and Tess by nuzzling them with his bony head, and Jamie was happy to see his backpack again.

'Are we safe?' Jamie whispered.

'Is that thing that was chasing us gone?'

They listened.

'I think so!' Tess breathed.

Thud!

The rocks shook.

'It's here!' Tess whispered.

Jamie peered up through the gap above his head. Instead of the trees of the jungle, he saw a dark slimy hole.

Suddenly, a blast of slime flew from the hole and splattered Jamie's face.

'Aargh!' Jamie wiped his face. 'I think that's its nose.'

The creature lifted its head and roared.

RAAAR!

The sound rumbled around the rocks.

Jamie could see its jaws. Pieces of rotting flesh dangled from its fangs.

'Ugh! Bad breath!' Jamie gagged. 'Worse than stinky ginkgo fruit.'

'It doesn't look friendly.'
Tess said. 'W–what is it?'

An enormous yellow eye, rimmed
with bright orange scales studied
Jamie through the gap in the rocks.

'D–don't n–need DinoData,' Jamie
stammered. 'It's a T–T–T. rex!'

CHAPTER 5

The eye disappeared.

'We're in trouble!' Jamie breathed.

'Serious trouble,' Tess said.

Suddenly, a long claw stabbed down into the crevice.

'Watch out!' Jamie yelled. He pulled Tess back and thrust his bag out as a shield. Wanna and Tess shrank back behind it.

The claw scratched and scrabbled around the gap in the rocks.

'It can't get us!' Tess whispered. 'Its arms are too short.'

'Maybe it will go away now,' Jamie said. But the huge unblinking eye of the T. rex reappeared.

Wanna trembled.

'If I had my stick,' Tess muttered, 'I'd
poke it in the eye!'

'There must be something we can use.'
Jamie groped in his backpack. 'Let's see
how it likes this.' Jamie pulled out his
flashlight and aimed it at the T. rex's eye.
He switched it on.

RAAAR!

The eye vanished. Cautiously, Jamie poked his head out of the crevice. The T. rex was stomping away into the jungle.

'Whew!' Jamie said. 'I think we're safe.'

They gave each other a high five.

'Now, let's get out of here,' Tess said, 'before it comes back!'

The two friends and the little dinosaur climbed out of the crevice, and Wanna took the lead again, heading farther downstream. 'Did you see that thing's teeth?' Jamie muttered as they splashed after their new dinosaur friend. 'That T. rex could rip us to shreds!'

'And eat us alive, bit by bit!' Tess shuddered.

Gradually, the stream grew wider and the trees on either side began to thin out. Soon, they had come to the edge of a lagoon that they had seen earlier from Ginkgo Hill. Wanna stopped near a large rock and began to munch on a leafy bush.

'We've come a long way from the cave,' Tess said. 'And there's a T. rex out to get us. How are we ever going to get back home?'

'I–I don't know…' Jamie gazed over the sparkling blue water.

Behind them, something started squawking.

Jamie and Tess whirled around. The squawks were coming from the yellow beaks of bat-like creatures in the palm tree. They looked like badly folded brown umbrellas, gripping the palm fronds with their scaly feet and the clawed fingers on their wings.

'They must be another type of pterosaur,' Tess decided.

Just then, the pterosaurs launched

themselves into the air, squawking and flapping their wings.

'What's up with them?' Tess asked as the birdlike creatures flew away.

The lagoon fell silent. The only sound was the water gently lapping the shore. Then, the ground began to shake.

'Uh-oh,' Jamie and Tess said together. 'The T. rex is back!'

CHAPTER 6

The T. rex sprang out of the jungle, sending up a spray of sand. Its orange stripes rippled in the sunshine as it scanned the beach.

Then, it saw them.

RAAAR!

The T. rex lowered its head. The
orange crests over its eyes flashed as it
stomped toward them.

'We're T. rex food,' cried Tess.

Then, suddenly, there was a sound of breaking branches behind them. The T. rex's head snapped up and it stared at the edge of the jungle.

Turning around slowly, Jamie saw a second T. rex crash out of the trees onto the beach.

'Oh no!' said Tess.

It was as big as the first, but darker, with black stripes. And it was advancing on them.

'Watch out!' Jamie rolled out of the way of a huge foot as the first T. rex stomped to meet the other T. rex.

Tess ducked as its tail swept over
her head.

They watched as the first T. rex hurled
itself at the newcomer.

'They're not after us!' he breathed.

'Maybe they're fighting over territory,'
Tess guessed.

The first T. rex sank its jaws into the other's throat. The dark T. rex screeched and writhed and thrashed its tail. Then it broke free, and lunged at the first T. rex's back. It hung on, biting its neck.

'Let's get out of here! Run!' Jamie dragged Tess toward the trees. Wanna bounded after them.

Gradually, the snarls and roars of the T. rex battle faded into the jungle sounds. The two friends stopped in a clearing, panting for breath.

'We're lost, aren't we?' Tess sat down on the ground and put her head in her hands. 'How are we going to get back?'

Grunk... grunk... grunk...

Wanna darted off into the trees.

'Maybe we could follow Wanna?' Jamie said. 'It's our best chance.'

After a moment, they were back at a stream. 'Is this the same stream as before?' Jamie wondered.

Next, Wanna led them down a jumble of rounded rocks.

'That's where we hid from the T. rex!' Tess grinned.

They passed the purple fungus and Jamie bent down and saw the 'W' on the tree stump. 'The Wanna tree!' he grinned.

Then, they climbed the slope through the ginkgo trees and, finally, they were standing in the mouth of the cave.

'That's how we got here!' Tess pointed to the fresh dinosaur footprint by the solid rock wall.

Wanna stood next to it, and wagged his tail. Then he stepped away, leaving two more identical footprints, but this time facing the rock.

'They're your footprints!' Jamie gasped.

Wanna blinked at him, turned and scurried into a pile of leaves and twigs piled up in the corner of the cave.

'He lives here! That's Wanna's nest!' Jamie rummaged in his backpack and took out the last ginkgo fruit.

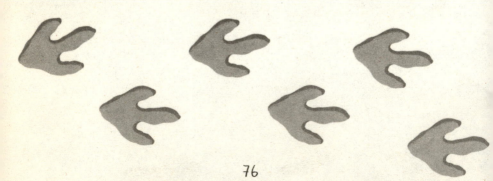

'This is for you, Wanna,' he said, putting it on the ground. 'Thank you for helping us.' Wanna's snout poked out of his nest. He nosed the fruit back to Jamie.

'I think he wants you to have it,' Tess said.

'Okay, Wanna,' said Jamie, picking it up. 'I'll put it in Mom's museum,' he told Tess, wrinkling his nose and smiling.

Tess was gazing at the rock with a puzzled expression on her face. 'We stepped forward to go back in time, so maybe we have to step backward to go forward in time,' she guessed.

Jamie nodded. 'I hope it works!'

Tess turned her back to the rock face.

Then she placed her right foot over
Wanna's print and stepped back with
her left. There was a flash of light
and Jamie found himself alone
with Wanna.

'It worked!' Jamie said to
Wanna. 'That means we can
come back and see
you again!'

He patted the
little dinosaur on
the snout. Wanna
nuzzled into Jamie's
hand, then curled

up in his nest.

'Goodbye, Wanna!' Jamie held the ginkgo fruit in one hand and his flashlight in the other. As he stepped back through the blaze of light, he felt the ground turn to stone beneath his feet. Then, he was back in the cave with Tess.

Jamie felt the ginkgo fruit in his hand soften. In the flashlight beam, he watched it shrivel and crumble to dust.

'We can't bring anything back,' he told Tess, letting the dust trickle between his fingers.

'It's just as well,' Tess said. 'That thing stank.'

The two friends squeezed through the hole in the rock, scrambled down the boulders, and hurried down the cliff path onto the beach.

Jamie's granddad was helping to pull a rowboat up onto the sand. He smiled at them and strode over.

'Did you find any dinosaurs?' he asked.

Jamie grinned at Tess. 'We found a fantastic cave, didn't we, Tess?'

'Awesome!' agreed Tess. 'Let's explore it some more tomorrow!'

'Great idea!' said Jamie, hoisting his backpack, and turning to his Granddad. 'If that's okay with you and Mom?'

'Just as long as you're not getting into any scrapes...' The Commander's eyes twinkled.

'See you tomorrow, Tess?' Jamie said
to his new friend. 'I'll message you later.'

'Sure thing!' Tess said as she
waved goodbye.

Jamie and Granddad walked back up
the path to the old lighthouse. Granddad
asked, 'You think you'll like living around
here, then?'

'Definitely!' said Jamie with a grin.
'I can't wait to tell the Dinosaur Club all
about it!'

Dinosaur timeline

The Triassic
(250–200 million years ago)

The first period of the Mesozoic Era was the Triassic.
During the Triassic, there were very few plants, and
the Earth was hot and dry, like a desert. Most of the
dinosaurs that lived during the Triassic were small.

The Jurassic
(200–145 million years ago)

The second period of the Mesozoic Era was the Jurassic.
During the Jurassic, the Earth became cooler and wetter,
which caused lots of plants to grow. This created a lot of
food for dinosaurs that helped them to grow big and thrive.

The Cretaceous
(145–66 million years ago)

The third and final period of the Mesozoic Era was the
Cretaceous. During the Cretaceous, dinosaurs were at
their peak and dominated the Earth, but at the end,
most of them suddenly became extinct.

Dinosaurs existed during a time on Earth known as the Mesozoic Era. It lasted for more than 180 million years, and it was split into three different periods: the Triassic, the Jurassic, and the Cretaceous.

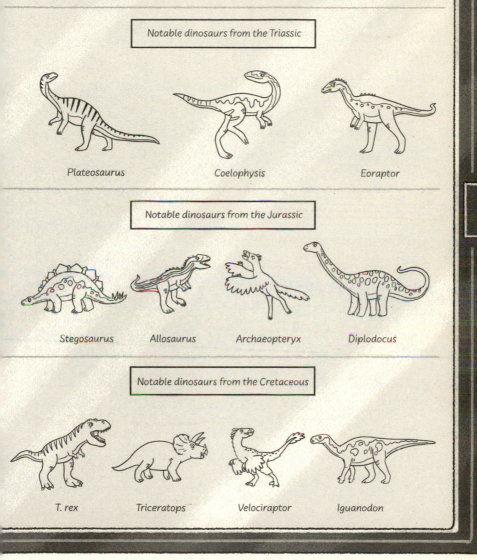

Notable dinosaurs from the Triassic

Plateosaurus

Coelophysis

Eoraptor

Notable dinosaurs from the Jurassic

Stegosaurus

Allosaurus

Archaeopteryx

Diplodocus

Notable dinosaurs from the Cretaceous

T. rex

Triceratops

Velociraptor

Iguanodon

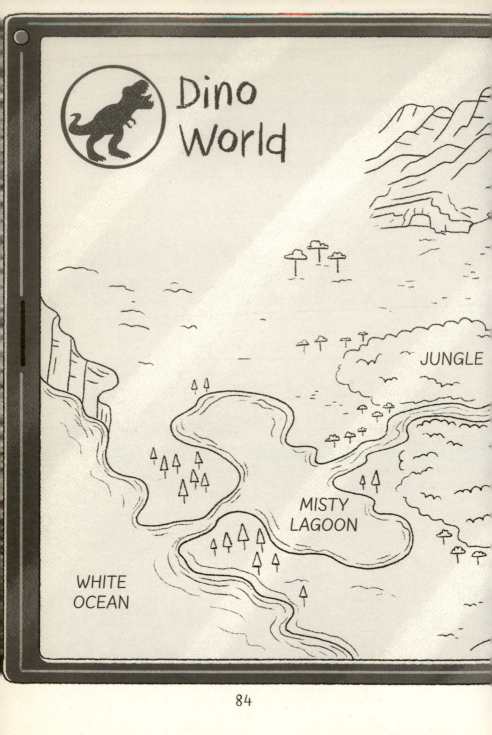

FARAWAY MOUNTAINS

CRASHING
ROCK
FALLS

FANG
ROCK

GREAT PLAINS

GINKGO
HILL

DINO
DATA

Also known as T. rex,
Tyrannosaurus was the
most powerful and dangerous
land predator of all time.
It is sometimes called
"King of the Dinosaurs."

Long tail
for balancing

Powerful legs

Name: Tyrannosaurus

Pronunciation: tie-RAN-oh-SORE-us

Period: Cretaceous

Size: 39ft (12m) long

Habitat: Forests and swamps

Diet: Meat

Huge head

Sharp teeth

Small arms

FACT

The name Tyrannosaurus
means "tyrant lizard."

DINO DATA

Wannanosaurus was a small dinosaur from the late Cretaceous period. It is known for having a very hard skull.

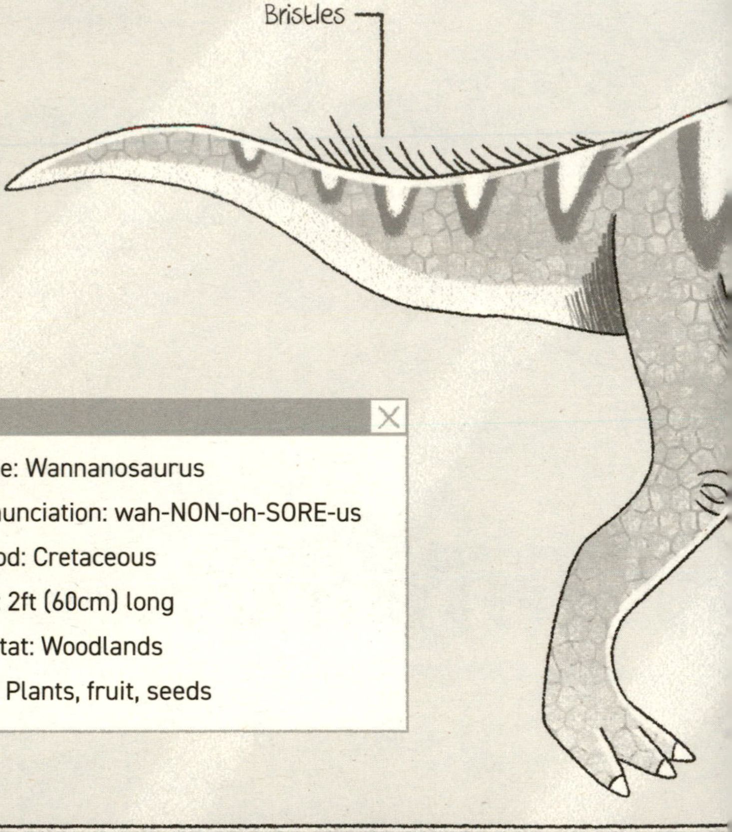

Bristles

Name: Wannanosaurus

Pronunciation: wah-NON-oh-SORE-us

Period: Cretaceous

Size: 2ft (60cm) long

Habitat: Woodlands

Diet: Plants, fruit, seeds

FACT

Wannanosaurus fossils were discovered in China.

Hard skull

FACT

Scientists aren't sure whether Wannanosaurus used its skull to defend itself from predators or to fight off rivals.

DINO DATA

Quetzalcoatlus was a pterosaur from the Cretaceous. About the size of a giraffe or a small plane, it was the largest animal ever to fly.

☒

Name: Quetzalcoatlus
Pronunciation: KWETS-ul-coe-AT-lus
Period: Cretaceous
Size: 36ft (11m) wingspan
Habitat: Plains
Diet: Small dinosaurs

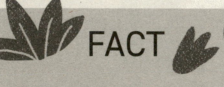

FACT

Pterosaurs weren't dinosaurs. They were flying reptiles that existed at the same time as dinosaurs.

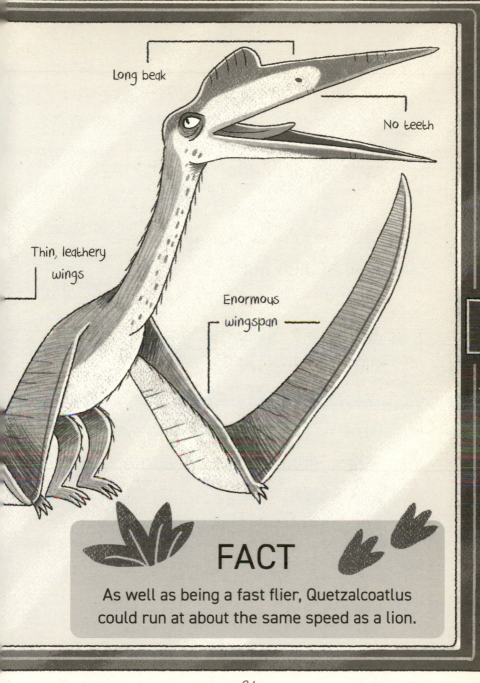

Long beak

No teeth

Thin, leathery
wings

Enormous
wingspan

FACT

As well as being a fast flier, Quetzalcoatlus
could run at about the same speed as a lion.

QUIZ

1   What type of dinosaur is Wanna?

2   True or false: A pterosaur was a
     type of dinosaur.

3   Which period of the Mesozoic Era
     did T. rex live in?

4   True or false: Quetzalcoatlus was the
     largest animal to ever fly.

5   What stinky fruit does Wanna like
     to eat?

6   True or false: T. rex was a meat-eater.

CHECK YOUR ANSWERS on page 95

GLOSSARY

AMMONITE
A type of sea creature that lived during the time of the dinosaurs

CARNIVORE
An animal that only eats meat

CRETACEOUS
The third period of the time dinosaurs existed (145–66 million years ago)

DINOSAUR
A group of ancient reptiles that lived millions of years ago

FOSSIL
Remains of a living thing that have become preserved over time

GINKGO
A type of tree that dates back millions of years

HERBIVORE
An animal that only eats plant matter

PALEONTOLOGIST
A scientist who studies dinosaurs and other fossils

PTEROSAUR
Ancient flying reptiles that existed at the same time as dinosaurs

PREDATOR
An animal that hunts other animals for food

QUIZ ANSWERS
1. Wannanosaurus
2. False
3. The Cretaceous
4. True
5. Ginkgo fruit
6. True

DK | Penguin Random House

Text for DK by Working Partners Ltd
9 Kingsway, London WC2B 6XF
With special thanks to Jane Clarke

Design by Collaborate Ltd
Illustrator Louise Forshaw
Consultant Emily Keeble

Acquisitions Editor James Mitchem
US Senior Editor Shannon Beatty
Senior Designer and Jacket Designer Elle Ward
Publishing Coordinator Issy Walsh
Production Editor Dragana Puvavic
Production Controller Isabell Schart
Publishing Director Sarah Larter

First American Edition, 2022
Published in the United States by DK Publishing
1450 Broadway, Suite 801, New York, New York 10018

Printed and bound in Great Britain by
Clays Ltd, Elcograf S.p.A.

www.dk.com
For the curious

The publisher would like to thank Jo Chukualim and Lynne Murray for
picture library assistance, and Caroline Twomey for proofreading.